This book belongs to

....

www.makebelieveideas.com

Written by Tim Bugbird.
Illustrated by Lara Ede.
Designed by Annie Simpson and Sarah Vince.

Clara
the Cookie Fairy

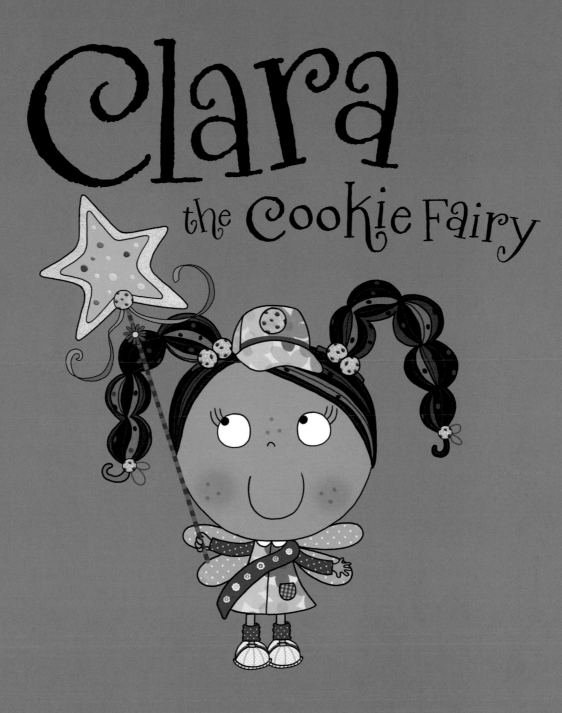

Tim Bugbird · Lara Ede

make believe ideas

Once there were three Fairy Scouts — Clara, Kat and Jan,
who lived upon a mountain in a fairy camper van.

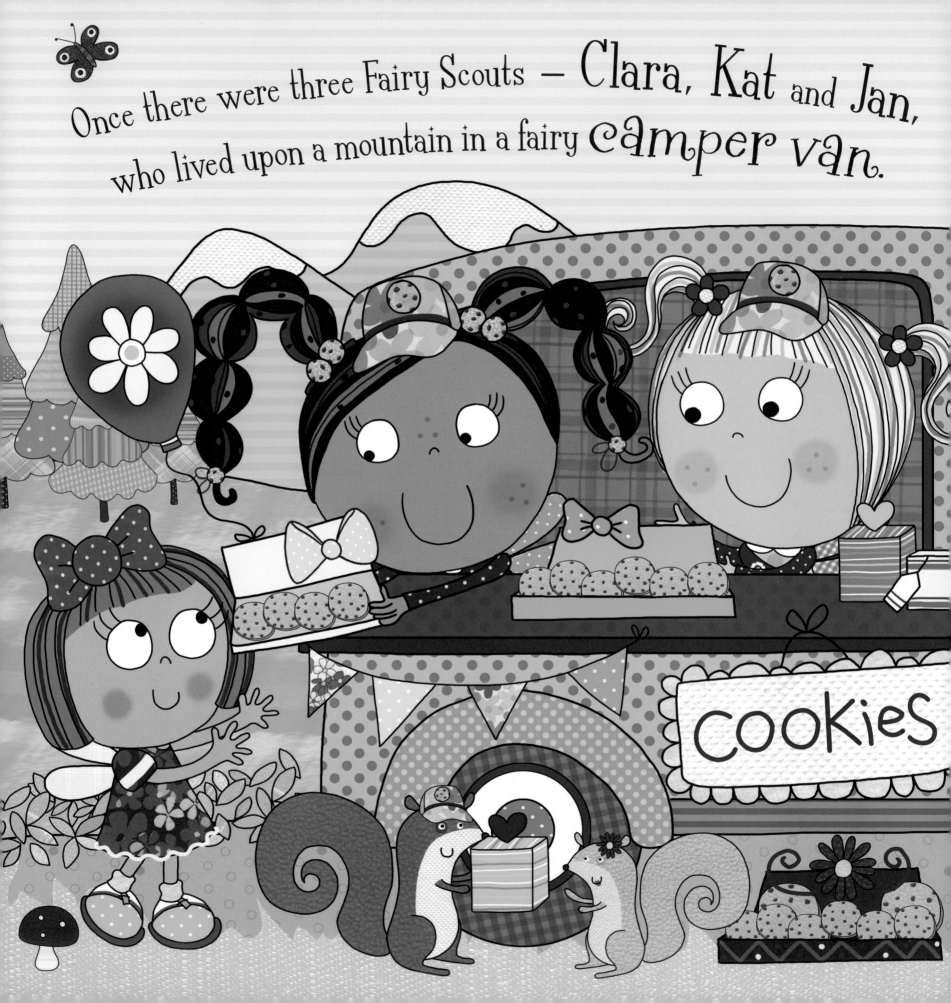

COOKIES

They sold special cookies – a Fairy-Scout tradition – to buy the things they needed for their camping expeditions!

Clara's wand made cookies, tasty, crisp and sweet,

and Kat's made **pretty** boxes
to keep them nice and **neat**.

Last of all, Jan's wand made a special fairy **bow**.
With every cookie **baked** and **boxed**, the friends were good to go!

Then, one summer's evening, they were driving out to dine, when Clara's eye was caught by a giant roadside sign.

The sign read:

MIGHTY MEGA-WANDS

make cookies with chocolate chips!

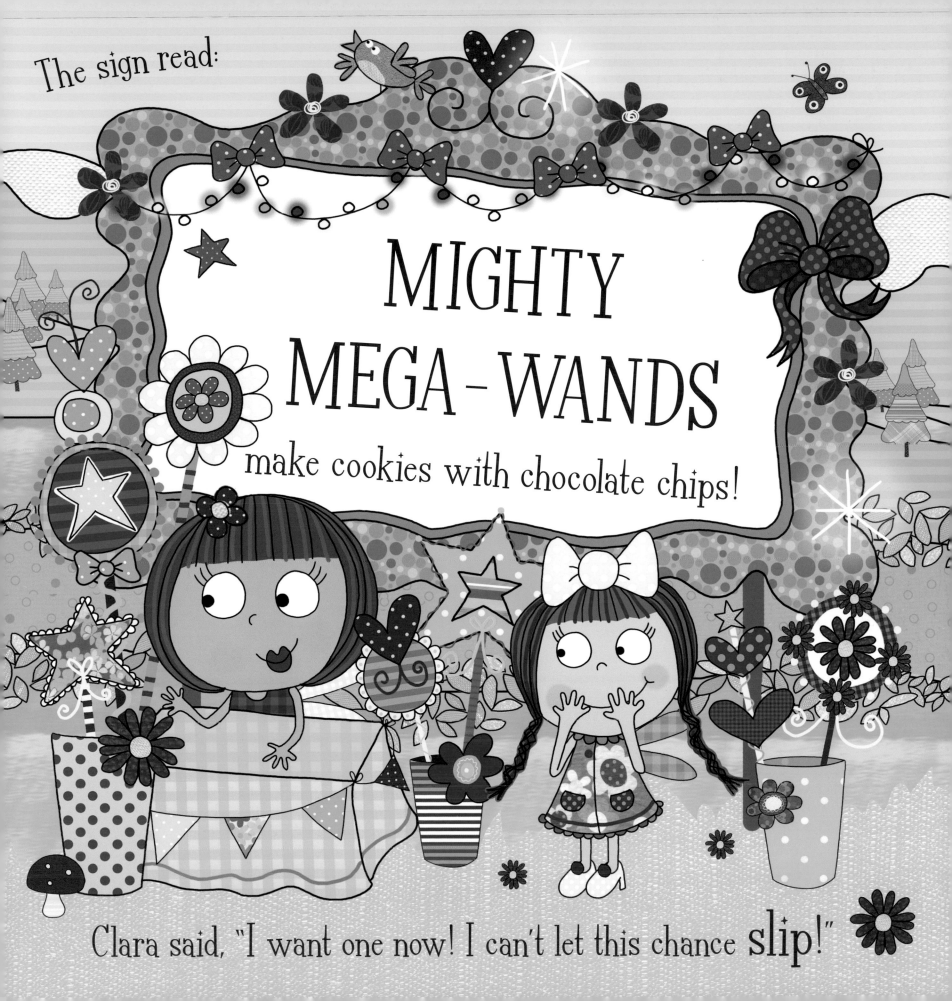

Clara said, "I want one now! I can't let this chance slip!"

Clara picked the biggest wand and stood in line to pay.
Her old one looked too boring so she threw it right away!

Pay here

But Clara **wasn't** careful and her wand was a little **brittle.**

She **whooshed**

and **swooshed** it way **too** much

and it **snapped** right in the middle!

The fairies tried to fix the wand
with string and tape and glue.
But not one thing would make it work.
Now what could they do?

glue

craft box

Kat said, "Only **one** thing will put us back on track —
we must find the **fairy dustcart**
and get your old wand **back!**"

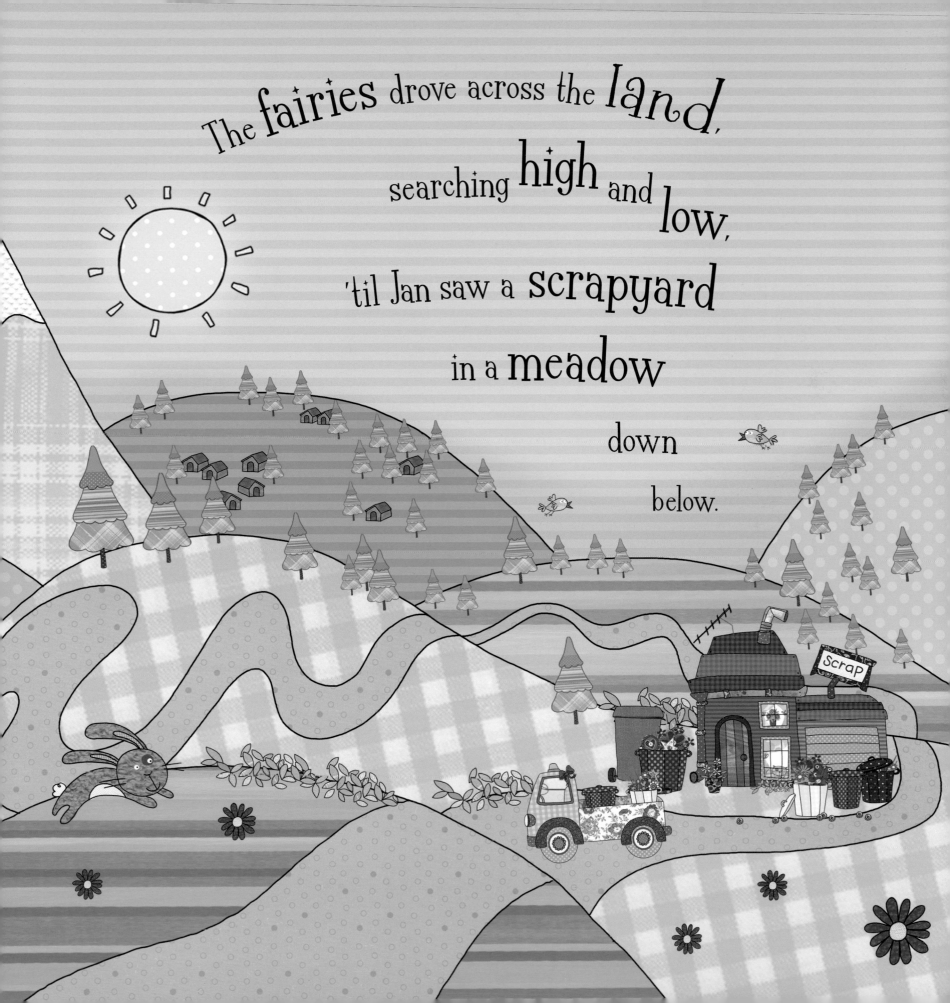

The fairies drove across the land,
searching high and low,
'til Jan saw a scrapyard
in a meadow
down
below.

"There's the **truck!**" cried Jan,
and she gave a little **cheer**.
"Let's fly down and look around.

Your **wand** just must be here!"

Unwanted wands were everywhere –
the place was overrun!
Lots looked just like Clara's,
so they tried them one by one.

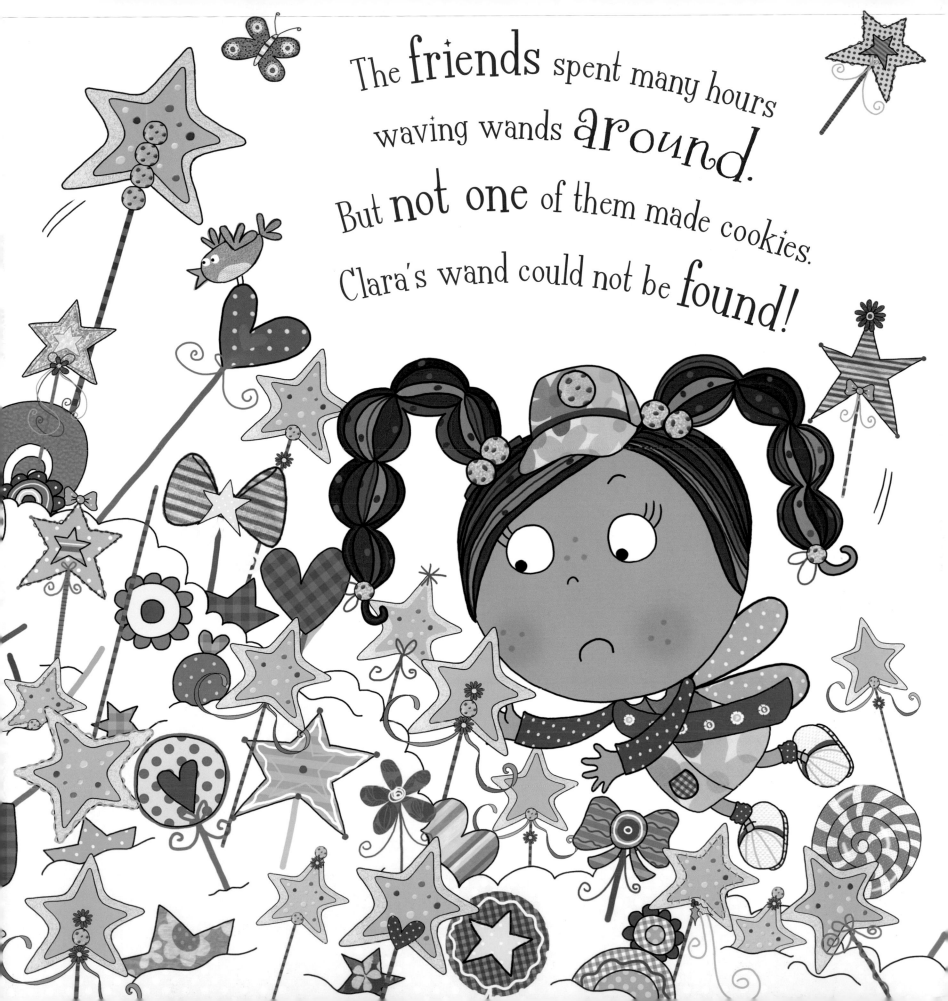

The **friends** spent many hours waving wands **around**.
But **not one** of them made cookies.
Clara's wand could not be **found**!

The fairies were getting **worried**.
Things weren't going well.

How would they fund their camping trip
if they had no cookies to sell?

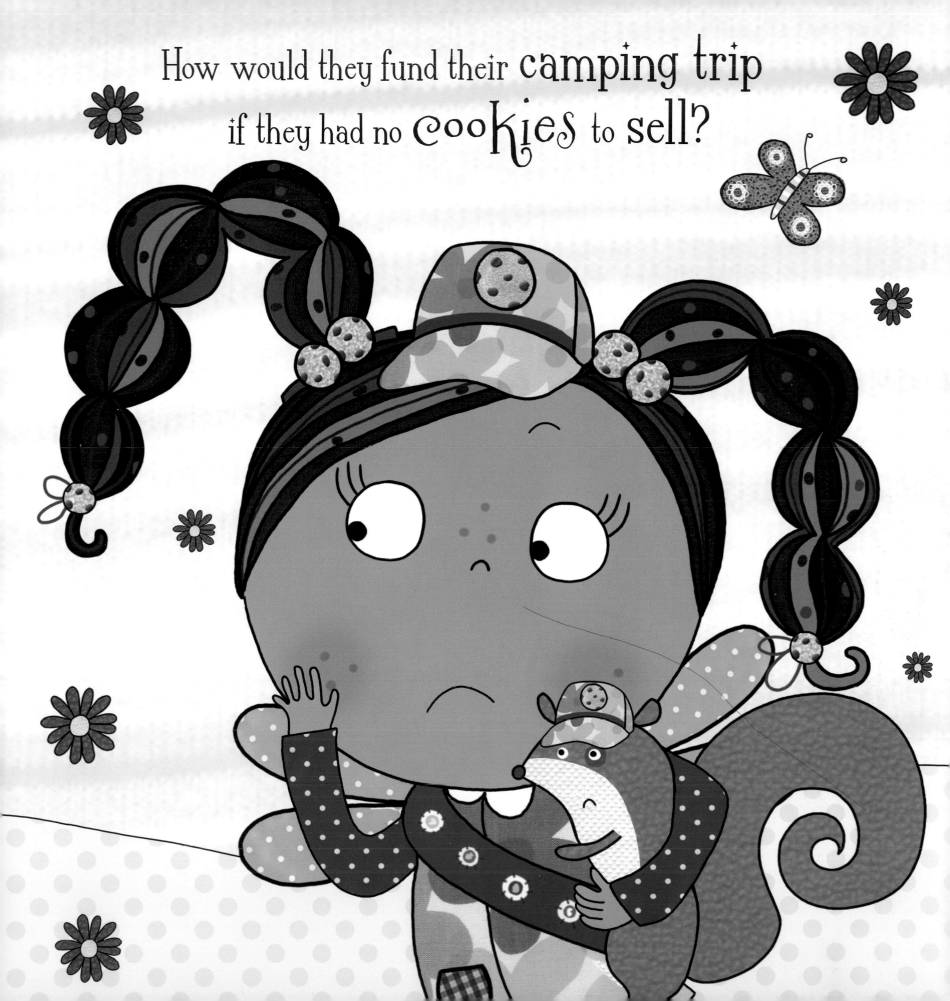

Then Clara said, "Stop! Look down!"
And suddenly it was clear.
What the wands had been making
was fairy camping gear!

There were
pots and pans,
forks and spoons,
kettles and cans
and guitars to play tunes!

There were balls and bats,
three fairy bikes,
bright summer hats
and boots for long hikes!

"These **wands** should be **used**,

not thrown away,"

said Clara with a frown.

"But if we put our heads together,

we can turn this **right around!**"

And in a **flash** it came to her,

a **new** Fairy-Scouting venture.

They'd move to the **meadow**

and transform the yard

into a **Swap and Recycling Centre!**

Fairies came from **far** and **wide**
with their **wands**, unwanted or broken,
to swap or make into something new.
The centre was **always** open!

And then one summer's day,
Clara had a huge surprise.
She waved the wand a fairy had found
and cookies fell from the skies!
"This is my wand!" cried Clara,
"And it works just as it should.

It's not a 'mighty mega-wand',
but to me it's twice as good!"

Clara learned to care for things, and not just throw them away.

To swap or recycle, if you can, is always the better way!